Why the Frog Has Big Eyes

Why the Frog Has Big Eyes

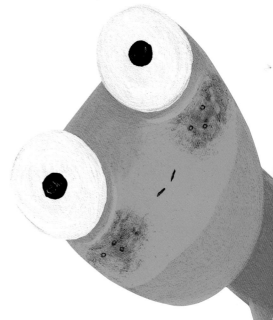

Betsy Franco

Illustrated by Joung Un Kim

Green Light Readers
Harcourt, Inc.

Orlando   Austin   New York   San Diego   London

Long ago, all frogs had small eyes.

One frog sat and stared all day.

"No one can stare as long as I can,"
Frog bragged.

His friends said, "Let's stop his bragging. Who can stare as long as Frog can?"

Horse trotted in.
"You will blink first," said Frog.
"I will not!" said Horse.

"See!" shouted Frog. "You did!"

Rabbit hopped in.
Rabbit didn't last long.
He blinked first.

"No one is better than I am!"
bragged Frog.